The RULERS

HEARTLESS

KINGDOM

K.I. LYNN

The RULERS

ATTICUS CHARLES DE LOUGHREY (1927–2020) — ELIZABETH (BARRET) DE LOUGHREY (1929–2003)

CHARLES DE LOUGHREY – VERA (ALDERIDGE) DE LOUGHREY

ATTICUS WILLIAM DE LOUGHERY (WICKED RULE)

ELIZABETH DE LOUGHREY (PRESTON) ALCOTT
   MADELINE
   BENNETT

HAMILTON DE LOUGHREY (RUTHLESS RULE)

PENELOPE DE LOUGHREY (TAINTED RULE)

GENEVIEVE DE LOUGHREY (WILD RULE)

HENRY DE LOUGHREY – VICTORIA (ROTHCHILD) DE LOUGHREY

RHYS DE LOUGHREY (LEATHAL RULE)

ADRIANNA DE LOUGHREY (DIED AT 15)

ATLAS DE LOUGHREY (DARK RULE)

SILAS DE LOUGHREY (DIRTY RULE)

GEORGIANA DE LOUGHREY (FORBIDDEN RULE)

KATHERINE (DE LOUGHREY) MONTGOMERY – WILLIAM MONTGOMERY JR.

WILLIAM MONTGOMERY III

ADELE MONTGOMERY

NATHANIEL MONTGOMERY

JAMES DE LOUGHREY
(DIED AT 27, NO CHILDREN)

HUGH DE LOUGHREY – CAROLINE (WHITNEY) DE LOUGHREY

JAMES

DANIELLA

ANNABELLE

JAQUELINE (TWIN TO JACKSON)

JAQUELINE DE LOUGHREY
(DIED AT 4 MONTHS)

THEN

Ten months ago…

The woman beneath me burned. Hot and wet. Each moan from her lips, each gasp as I drove deeper into her, sent a jolt down my spine.

Finding myself looking down into the irresistible eyes of the blonde siren was not the outcome I had expected when I went out for drinks with my cousin to one of the posh clubs that he owned. I didn't pick women up often, and when I did, I certainly didn't take them home.

Well, not home exactly. To a hotel I owned.

A few hours earlier, I'd begrudgingly stepped across a threshold and into the cesspool known as a nightclub. Immediately my skin prickled, and I fought the urge to turn around and retreat to my sanctuary, but an arm dropping down onto my shoulder halted me.

"Don't even think about it, cousin," Rhys said, pulling me through the crowd and the sea of gyrating bodies.

The music thumped loudly as we passed the speakers, making my head pound in time.

"This isn't necessary," I said as we approached the velvet rope at the base of a set of stairs where a security guard kept watch.

"Good evening, Omar!" Rhys said with a jovial smile.

The guard smiled back. "Evening, Mr. de Loughrey," he replied, then unhooked the rope and moved aside. "Have a good time."

"That's the plan," Rhys called back as we ascended the stairs to the VIP section.

After a long, hard battle of a week, all I wanted to do was sink into my bed and not move for a few hours, but, as usual, my wants were never a consideration.

"Relax. We're here to enjoy the evening and maybe the company of a lady or two. Maybe three, if we're lucky."

Club rats were not my taste, but that didn't mean I couldn't enjoy the view.

We entered the private space filled with couches and a table hidden by large, heavy curtains. Shortly after, a barely dressed waitress came in and took our order.

"Would you relax?"

I narrowed my gaze at him. "Said the snake."

"To the lion. If anyone is eating anyone, it's you."

I blew out a breath and rubbed my hands across my stubble.

"We need to celebrate."

"It's been six months," I argued.

He rolled his eyes. "Six months since you've been CEO, and not once have you celebrated that accomplishment."

"It's hard to celebrate something that I always knew was going to be mine."

"It's still an accomplishment. You didn't get it simply because you are the firstborn. You worked your ass off to climb to the top."

He was right. From a young age, it was drilled into me that I needed to be the best and that only the best would lead the de Loughrey legacy into the future. If I failed to rise to the top, the mantle would have been passed to whoever was worthy.

The music drew me to the railing, and I surveyed the crowd, watching the pulsing lights beat in time with the bass thumping from the speakers. It was too loud for my tastes, but Rhys was correct—I needed to celebrate.

For years I'd sacrificed everything in my climb to the top— to the point that the company was my life. Every minute of the day was spent thinking about the many workings of our near two-hundred-year-old family business. We'd come out unscathed in the battles of the Industrial Revolution, survived the Great Depression, and exploded in the Technological Age.

"Are those grey hairs I see in all that dark blond?" Rhys said, forcing me to acknowledge his close proximity.

I narrowed my gaze as I turned toward him. His grey eyes sparkled with mirth. They were the same eyes as my younger brother, Hamilton. The same as my father and uncle, as well as my grandfather.

The eyes of a predator.

An interesting observation.

My own were blue, like my mother—warm enough to draw one in, cool enough to give one pause, and calculating enough to frighten even the strongest of constitutions.

"No more than those cropping up in your dark locks. You need a haircut."

Rhys ran his hand through his hair which seemed a few weeks past the point of needing a trim. "All the better to be gripped and tugged on when I'm between a woman's thighs."

A notion he wasn't incorrect about. My scalp tingled with the desire for just that.

"I bet we could find something pretty to top your evening off with."

"It would be easier to simply call Bridget or Antonia." The two women were often called upon as dates to events or for an evening when I was in need of relief.

"Where is the fun and excitement in that? The thrill of some nimble, nubile young woman to warm your cock?"

Sadly, his mere description awakened the craving for all that he depicted.

"Where do you find the energy?"

"For starters, my brain isn't hardwired to the company twenty-four seven. Second, I don't waste *all* of my excess energy in the gym. Third, I enjoy the hunt. A hungry cock will do whatever is necessary to dive into the wet warmth of young, tight pussy."

"You do realize you're starting to sound like Hamilton."

He shrugged. "I'm not as...virile as he is. My appetite is more refined, and I don't pursue it every week. Besides, the brainless bimbos he usually beds hold little appeal to me. I prefer the chase."

"I'm here to relax."

"And nothing is more relaxing than coming into a woman's mouth up here with hundreds of bodies mere feet below."

"I'll take that under advisement."

He sighed and leaned against the rail.

"If you don't want to put forth the effort, just tell them who you are. I've had women clamoring over each other to get on my dick after they heard my last name. Everyone knows the de Loughrey name. We're a fucking American icon."

Before I could compose a retort, the waitress arrived with our drinks, and I gladly took a few hard sips of the amber liquid.

As I did, I watched as a woman with short blonde hair stepped off the dance floor and headed toward the bar. She seemed a bit out of place, which caught my eye. While most women were in tight, body-hugging, bust-enhancing scraps of fabric, the skirt of her dress fluttered behind her. It was more the dress of a garden party than a night out.

The deep navy contrasted against her pale skin, and something white danced across the fabric, breaking up the monotony.

No one followed her, and she found an empty seat at the far end of the bar. As I conversed with Rhys, I periodically glanced her way, and not a soul ever approached.

After finishing my drink, I glanced back to find her still on her own.

All of Rhys's talk of the chase—and a little relaxation from the liquor—had my mind spinning.

"I'm going to go get a refill."

His brow furrowed. "Cindy will be back in a few."

I cleared my throat as I stood. "It's fine."

He shook his head. "The bar is a mess. I wouldn't."

"I'll return," I said, not waiting for a response as I pushed through the heavy curtains and made my way down the dark hallway.

An odd thump of my heart pounded as I descended the stairs and caught a closer look at her. She seemed to be sipping a clear glass of something. Gin and tonic, perhaps?

There was something out of place about her, more than her unearthly quality. She was dressed for the evening, somewhat conservatively compared to other women, with the skirt of her dress loose and hitting mid-thigh, and her inhibitions appeared not to have been taxed by alcohol. Her attention was on the wall behind the bartender and my curiosity piqued even more, almost desperate to know what was on her mind. The curiosity drew me ever closer.

"What's the celebration?" I asked. The words were out before I even realized I'd leaned in.

She jumped and turned toward me, her brown eyes wide. I usually wasn't attracted to women with short hair, but the long pixie cut seemed to suit her. High cheekbones, large eyes, flawless skin, and perfectly pink, kissable lips were featured on her oval face.

"Forgive me. I didn't mean to startle you."

She blinked and smiled as she shook her head. "No, I'm sorry, I was spacing out. What was the question?"

"What are you celebrating?"

She sighed and attempted a smile. "It's my birthday."

I scrunched my brow. "Why do you look so down about that?"

She stared down at the glass in her hand. "Honestly, I'm questioning what the fuck I'm doing here."

I glanced around and took note of how she failed to follow, searching out no one. "Please don't say you're here alone."

She looked away and swallowed. "Everyone was busy."

I leaned back. There was something about her that drew me in closer, something that wouldn't allow me to leave her by herself—my little sea nymph, sitting on her rock all alone.

I held out my hand. "Come with me."

"What?" She looked down at my offered hand.

A chuckle left me. "I have a table. We will help you celebrate."

She shook her head. "Thanks, but I think I'm just going to go home."

"I insist." I gained the bartender's attention and called him over.

"Yes, sir. What can I do for you?"

"Can you send her drink up along with a bourbon, neat?"

"Yes, sir." He took her drink, despite her protest.

"And whatever her tab is, deal with it."

"Yes, sir."

"What are you doing?" she asked with wide eyes.

I cleared my throat and glanced down at my hand. With a huff, she took it and I reveled in the warmth of her touch as she slid off her stool, her purse tucked into her other hand. Once she was on her feet, I slipped her hand into the crook of my arm and led her away. When we reached the staircase, the music lessened as we retreated from the speakers. The bodyguard standing there gave me a nod and moved to the side to allow us up.

"What's your name?"

"Ophelia."

"Ophelia. That's a beautiful name. Mine is Atticus."

"Where are we going? The tables are down there." She pointed over her shoulder, an edge of apprehension in her tone.

Hoping to put her at ease that I had nothing nefarious up my sleeve, I gave her a warm smile, something few people ever received from me. "The VIP section."

Her lips parted and her eyes widened. We finished the climb and moved into a dimly lit walkway with large, thick curtains on one side. Once we reached the middle, I parted the curtains and ushered her through.

Rhys's gaze was wide as he eyed the woman coming into the private space.

"What's this?" he asked, his lips pulling up into a grin. I very much noticed the glint in his eye and the "I told you so" smirk that formed.

"Ophelia," she said as she held out her hand. Rhys, being as lethal as ever, took her hand in his and kissed the top.

"What did I do to be graced with such a beauty?"

She quirked a brow at him. "Does that line actually work?"

I burst out laughing, surprising both of them. "I told you, your lines are over the top, and here I am, proven correct."

"What did he say to get you up here?" he asked her, then

glared at me. "And my lines warm my bed every night I desire without fail."

"He didn't say much, just to follow him."

"So direct, Atticus. It's shocking."

I narrowed my gaze at him as I sipped on the drink the waitress had set down. "I find speaking directly works."

"Ophelia, answer me this: does flattery not work on you? Atticus is quite brash and often called insensitive by women, and you have me curious."

"It wasn't really words, but I'm also not sure I understand the undercurrent of associating me with him. Yes, he convinced me to come with him, but that doesn't make me his."

Rhys leaned in closer. "Does that mean you'd be mine for the night?"

"No."

I smirked at the lack of hesitation. She wasn't falling for him.

"Why not?"

"You're shady as fuck," she said without pause.

I couldn't contain my laughter again. What the hell was going on with me? Rhys's confusion at my reaction was evident in his wide-eyed stare.

"He has laughed twice now. I'm going to have to ask you to take him back down and return with the correct Atticus, but before that, why such a harsh comparison?" Rhys's wounded pride was bleeding all over the place.

"It's in your attitude. The vibe you give off."

"And by that, you trust him more than me?" Rhys was both seriously affronted and entertained. Given that I was known as the wicked king, I found it interesting that she held even an inkling of trust for me.

"She has good intuition. Lethal lawyers are shady as fuck."

He narrowed his eyes at me. "Might I remind you that it is a shadiness you have used to your advantage more than once."

I tipped my glass to him. "True. However, we aren't talking about a business venture, but the company of a woman."

"What are you boys doing up here all alone?" she asked, putting an end to our spat.

Rhys leaned back. "Trying to let loose after a hard week."

I scoffed. While Rhys was normally reserved and cut-throat, he also had a playful nature about him. He was more social than me, but I knew why he pounded back the drinks, and why he wore a façade. I saw the dark emptiness, if even just a flicker.

"What do you do, Ophelia?" I asked, curious about the little nymph beside me.

"Right now, I'm a waitress."

I'd hoped she'd be something a little more interesting to help explain her appeal. Still, it failed to tamp down my curiosity.

"Right now?" Rhys asked with a quirk of his brow.

She nodded. "I have a degree in biology and was briefly in pharmaceutical sales, but that didn't work out. I just haven't found what I want to do yet."

That was more interesting. At least she was intelligent.

"What do you do?" she asked as she looked at me. There seemed to be a current moving that I hadn't noticed before, and I quite enjoyed the simmer of heat that pulsed between us.

I glanced to Rhys, then gave her a strained smile. I didn't want to tell her. It would ruin the atmosphere. I was genuinely enjoying our time.

"I went into the family business. Boring stuff."

"Didn't have a choice?"

My jaw clenched. "Not really."

"From the day he was born, his future was set," Rhys said, covering the truth and redirecting her attention on the subject.

"And what about you? Lawyer, was it?"

Rhys grinned. "Corporate lawyer."

Nothing about his answer was untrue, just the omission of it being the family company.

"Remind me, is that better or worse than an ambulance chaser?" she asked.

Another laugh burst from me. What had gotten into me? I wasn't one to show enjoyment in anything. Something about my little nymph was drawing it out of me.

Despite what she said, she *was* mine, if even just for the night.

"You wound me, Ophelia."

She smiled and shook her head. "I doubt there is little that would wound you. What did Atticus call you? The Lethal Lawyer?"

"I do like them feisty."

She shrugged, then turned to me. "How about you?"

My heart thrummed roughly in my chest as her brown eyes bored into mine.

"Feisty or not, it makes no difference. I'm enjoying your company regardless."

She settled back against the couch, her shoulders settling under my arm. The current intensified, firing off tingles across every inch of her that rested against me.

"He wins."

Perhaps I would be taking someone home this evening.

OPHELIA

The alcohol warmed me, but not as much as the man I'd inched my way closer to over the past hour. Despite the way the evening began, I thoroughly enjoyed myself with these two gorgeous strangers in a VIP booth at Angelino.

It was one of the hottest clubs in the city, and I only came out on the invitation from my friend Jennifer.

Who then cancelled on me last minute. Whatever. We'd barely talked over the last few years, but she saw a post on Facebook and invited me.

Still, I came, using her name, which was on the list—I guess dating a professional baseball player had its advantages—and cutting the line of people hoping to cross the threshold.

I had been two sips from walking out, ending the night early, when Atticus appeared beside me. His blue eyes held me in thrall, his voice on edge, and those were only the first two things I noticed about the man.

There was a dusting of stubble accentuating his strong jaw, and he had a straight nose, perfectly styled light brown—possibly dirty blond—hair, with similarly colored brows that shadowed his intense gaze.

His lips.

Immediately my body flamed red-hot just imagining his lips ghosting across my skin. I forced myself to look away and focus on the charcoal-colored suit that hugged his body in the most perfect way.

When I took his hand, I was pleasantly surprised by his height. At five-and-a-half feet tall, pretty close to six-feet in heels, he was still inches above me.

Two hours later, I was as entranced by his eyes, his lips, and his body as I had been when I first saw him. His voice left me wet and wanting from the beginning. I'd just returned to the VIP lounge from a trip to the bathroom, where I'd removed my thong and shoved it into the pocket of my dress, preferring the cool air to the damp sensation.

When I pushed through the heavy curtain, I was greeted by Atticus's warm smile.

"You didn't run off."

I quirked a brow at him. "Is that code for I should have left?"

He stood and stepped toward me as I moved to the railing. Rhys had disappeared while I was away, leaving us alone with the heavy crackling of attraction that pulled us together.

I swallowed hard and looked out over the crowd, trying to tamp down the lustful thoughts I was having about the gorgeous man.

My hips swayed to the beat as I let my mind go and lost

myself. A gasp left me as my skin electrified, and I slowed the roll of my hips.

Atticus's strong chest was against my back, his arms on either side of me, caging me against the railing. The warmth of his body muddled my mind. The heat of his breath against my neck followed by the light brush of his lips and stubble had me pushing back into him.

"I don't do this, ever, but I have a hotel room a few blocks away. I would hate for the evening to end," he said against my ear, his voice a low, gravelly tone, deep and rich, that sent shivers down my spine.

Every word the man said held an air of power, and his voice projected confidence.

I'd never had a one-night stand, yet with the tangible chemistry between me and the man behind me, I had a feeling that was about to change.

"It would be a first for me," I said as I arched my neck and leaned back against him.

He let out a low groan before lightly nipping my neck just below my ear, sending a jolt through my system.

"Is that a yes?" He rocked his hips against my ass, and my mouth popped open at the feel of his hard length pressing against me.

I moved my hips, grinding against him for a moment before twisting to look at him. His eyes were dark, lips only a few inches away. Craning my neck, I nipped at his bottom lip, then ran my tongue against it to soothe the sting, loving the way his gaze darkened.

"Yes."

He reached up and gripped my jaw, holding me in place as his lips pressed fiercely against mine. "Let's go."

Rhys entered just as we were exiting, surprise on his face morphing into a knowing smirk.

"Have a good night," he said with a wink.

"Good night. Thanks for the fun," I said as Atticus pulled me out and down the hallway.

His demeanor was almost frenzied with the way he bulldozed through the crowd, but when we made it outside to the street, he relaxed.

"I didn't want to lose you," was all he said as he slowed to a more manageable pace.

My hand was warm in his as we walked a few blocks down to Le Magnifique, a five-star hotel that I could never afford to stay in.

His touch was forceful in a desperate sort of way, one that fueled the fire inside me with each bit of movement. He couldn't seem to let go of my hand. And the farther we walked, the tighter he gripped me. Was he afraid I was going to change my mind? As if there was a choice in the matter.

I'd never been more drawn to a man. Nor had I ever been more desperate to feel one's lips or body on mine.

Somehow, we managed not to maul each other in the elevator, but we were barely through the door when he pushed me against the wall, his lips crashing to mine. The fire that had started the moment I looked up into his sapphire eyes exploded into a raging inferno, burning every vein as my blood moved through my body.

He held my jaw tight, his thumb and fingers digging in

as he devoured my mouth, his other hand fisting the back of my hair, threading through the shorter ends as he tried to possess me.

His tongue created a spiraling shock that moved through me, and I was trapped in the gravity of him too far to notice his fingers pulling at the tie on the back of my dress until the top slipped down and fabric pooled low on my hips.

A light pull at the zipper and my dress was a puddle of fabric at my feet.

"No panties?" he growled.

"I lost them."

"Lost them?"

"Yes. They were wet from being so close to you."

A groan left him and the intensity rolling off him increased. "Tell me why."

My fingers flexed against his chest and I bit down on my bottom lip. "Because every word out of your mouth goes straight to my clit."

His lips tugged up into a smug smile.

"You seem to have lost all of your clothing," he said, his gaze traveling all the way down, sending a blaze of heat across my skin as he went.

"Your fault again. I think you wanted to see me naked."

His hand slipped between my thighs, and I gasped as his fingers slid against my clit, then down until he had two fingers buried inside me. A high-pitched cry left me, my muscles tense from the sudden explosion of pleasure.

"I think you may be right. Do you want to know what I

know?" he asked. My eyes glazed over, lips parting as his fingers moved in and out, sliding across my clit as he did.

"W-what's that?"

He pried my mouth open and slipped his thumb in, which I instantly lapped at, earning a strained groan. "That you will look exquisite when you come on my cock."

I reached forward and gripped his bulge, earning a low rumble from his chest and a harder drive of his fingers.

Fuck, he was thick.

He tilted my head back, his thumb slipping from my mouth just as his teeth scraped across the length of my neck.

Complete control was his, and it felt so good.

"You know what will look great as well?" I asked. Each breath reached higher in pitch as he drove me closer and closer to orgasm.

He kissed and nipped his way up to my ear before biting lightly on my earlobe. "What's that?"

I turned my head so that I could get closer to his ear, and his hand dropped down to rest lightly on my neck.

"My lips wrapped around your cock," I whispered, giving him a squeeze. He groaned, then bit down on my neck before his touch vanished from my body.

A whimper left me, but when I looked into his eyes, the predator that looked back sent a jolt of excitement through my system.

"On your knees." He removed his suit jacket before working open his belt and then his slacks. By the time my knees hit the marble floor, I was at eye level. It had been a while since I'd been up close and personal with a man, but I didn't remember ever being as intimidated before.

My whole body flushed in anticipation, and I reached out. He was warm, heavy, and thick. I wasn't some petite little thing, but even my fingers couldn't encircle his girth. My pussy clenched in anticipation of having him inside me, *filling* me, *stretching* my walls.

I looked up at his dark eyes that watched me. He reached out and gripped my jaw again before slipping his thumb into my mouth.

"Suck it, just like that," he growled before releasing me.

Leaning forward, I ran my tongue along the underside of his shaft, flicking the tip before closing my lips around the head. I worked my way down, loving each sigh and low vocalization that slipped from him.

"You're right. You are a vision with your mouth stuffed full of my cock."

I released him and dipped lower, my tongue circling one of his balls before sucking it into my mouth. Another curse hissed through clenched teeth, and I repeated the action on the other side as I pumped his length before returning to swallow as much as I could, starting at the head.

"Fuck, you're good at that." He pushed on the back of my head, and I choked, unable to go as far as he wanted.

Another low growl vibrated deep in his chest and he pulled me up to my feet. A gasp left me as he delivered a painful but pleasurable slap to my clit before he stepped forward and grabbed my ass.

His fingers dug into my butt cheeks as he lifted me up, my legs instinctively wrapping around his waist.

"You have a fantastic ass. I'm going to enjoy fucking you from behind and watching it bounce as you take my cock."

"Promises, promises," I said before nipping his neck. A growl rumbled in his chest before I was shocked by a sting across my butt before he started walking toward the bedroom.

I felt the hot head of his cock tapping against me with each step. A few more steps, and my stomach flipped as we fell onto the bed. His lips smashed to mine, and I was lost in the intoxicating hunger with which he possessed me.

He pulled back and I let out a whine, earning me another tap on my clit. "You are a needy little nymph," he said as he pulled at his clothes. His tie went first, followed by his vest, dress shirt, and undershirt before he finally removed everything from his lower half.

The suit that looked painted on only hid the body of a god beneath the rich fabrics. Lean, taut muscles, strong, broad chest and shoulders, defined abs, and even that heavenly, groan-inducing *V*. The man was perfection of the male species.

I reached down to pull off my heels, but his hand grasped mine, stopping me.

"Leave those on for now." He gripped my breast, drawing my nipple between his fingers and tugging, making me cry out. "Mmm, I like that sound."

He retreated again before pulling a condom from the bedside drawer and putting it on. My thighs rubbed together as I bit down on my lip, entranced by the flawless specimen before me.

I scooted back up the bed as he closed in. With strong hands, he pushed my thighs open, licking his lips as he stared down at my pussy.

He smacked his cock against my clit, making me jump and grind my hips against him as he positioned himself.

"Here's one promise for you," he said, then slammed his hips against mine. I lost all thought as he drove in, filling me in a way I didn't think I ever had been. My eyes fluttered, and my mouth fell open as he stretched me. His lips were against my ear, but I was still lost in the initial shock and pleasure. "I'm going to fuck you so hard, that you won't be able to walk when I'm done."

The pace he set up was hard and unrelenting, my back arching under his assault. His lips were fire and sin, and I burned under their touch.

"Atticus," I whimpered, my head thrown back.

"You feel so fucking good," he groaned. He lavished my neck with liquid fire, drowning me in desire while begging for more. I lost the ability to think, consumed by pleasure with every thrust as he pushed me higher and higher into ecstasy.

"Look at me," he growled. One hand gripped my jaw again, tilting my head where he wanted.

I forced my eyes open, instantly losing myself in the intensity of his gaze.

The guttural groans coming from him had me squeezing around him even harder. His thrusts became more aggressive, faster, and a scream left me as every muscle tensed, then let go.

"That's it, fucking come," he snarled.

I barely registered the last hard slams of his hips against mine, but I felt every twitch of his cock inside me.

His breath was hard and harsh against my neck, and I knew mine was the same.

Wow.

Never had a guy done to me the things Atticus had just done. For one, I came. Hard. And I felt like it was just a promise of more to come.

For another, the chemistry was off-the-charts hot.

After a few minutes, he pulled back, a relaxed grin on his face. I whimpered when he pulled out, missing the full feeling of having him inside me.

He stood and pulled off the condom before throwing it in the trash.

"Water?" he asked as he headed through the door.

"Yes, please." I rolled over in time to watch his sinful ass walk away.

Happy Birthday to me!

The night had done a complete one-eighty compared to how I thought it would go when I left my apartment.

When he returned, he handed me a bottle of water, which I greedily downed as he sat next to me. The room service menu was in his hand, and he opened it before passing it to me.

"I'm hungry. You?"

I blinked at him. "I kinda worked up an appetite."

"Get whatever you want. You'll need the calories."

A shiver zipped down my spine at the rough edge of his voice. "I will?"

He smirked. "I'm not done with you yet."

"Really?" I asked as I bit down on my lip and scanned the menu. A sigh of disappointment fell over me. "They don't have much this late."

"Whatever you want. Don't worry about the time."

"What makes you so special?" I asked, curious where his confidence came from.

"We're in the penthouse. Trust me."

It was then it really hit me—we *were* in the penthouse.

Sometime in the early morning hours, we had both succumbed to exhaustion and fallen asleep. When I woke, I found I was snuggled into Atticus's side, my head on his chest, legs wrapped with his.

Tilting my head back, I found blue eyes looking at me and felt the soft caress of fingers across my back.

"Good morning."

My face burned, and I looked away. "Good morning."

The situation felt like he would have kicked me out when done, and I would have been doing the walk of shame back to the train station, but that wasn't what happened at all. While I didn't expect, nor want, any declarations of anything, I immensely enjoyed the peace that moved between us, light and airy, while the warmth of his skin against mine settled into my affection-starved bones.

"How do you feel?" he asked, his fingers never faltering in their caress.

"A little sore, but good. You?"

"Hungry."

I looked back up and met his gaze. The brightness had dimmed, overtaken by a darkness. The intense moment was cut short by his stomach grumbling beneath my hand.

I couldn't help but laugh, and neither could he. "What do you want first?"

"Move your hand down a little more, and I think you'll figure it out."

"Bathroom first." I pulled away from him, instantly missing his warmth as I dashed to relieve myself. Once done, I found Atticus walking in, heading to the sink where he picked up a toothbrush. Looking to the other sink, I noticed a complimentary toothbrush and followed suit, giving my mouth a quick cleaning.

When he was done, he moved to the massive shower and turned it on. I couldn't keep my eyes off his cock as it bobbed about, hard and needy and completely hypnotizing, especially after the night's events.

He pulled me into the shower with him, pressing my back against the cold tiles. Just as the night before, he picked me up, my legs wrapping around him as the warm water crashed down on us. He teased me with his lips, ghosting them across mine before pulling back, a smirk greeting me. Before he could do it again, I cupped his face and pulled his lips to mine.

What started out as a languid consumption quickly escalated into a ravaging. And I loved every second. A ragged sigh left me when I felt the head of his cock push through my pussy lips, and I sank down on his length.

That seemed to morph his frenzy into a slow, sensual thrusting.

"You are absolutely divine."

Though sore from our night, a slow burn grew, intensifying with each thrust.

"I want to come," he hissed, looking down to where we were connected before finding my eyes again. He reached between us and brushed his fingers across my clit. We both moaned, and his teeth clenched.

"Come, Ophelia." The pressure of his fingers increased with the speed of his thrusts. "I need you to come, baby."

My thighs shook as I clenched down around him, my head tilted back into a scream. His teeth dug into my neck, and he groaned as he pulled out, his cock pulsing as his cum shot out, landing on my breasts and stomach.

As we came down, I reached up and brought his forehead down to mine. "Where did you come from?"

He chuckled and pressed his lips to mine. "Come on, let's clean up."

Once we were washed and I was dried off, I wobbled toward the door to determine where my dress had been deposited. There was a chuckle behind me as I braced myself against the wall.

"Yeah, yeah, job well done."

He chuckled again. "I'm known for being an overachiever."

With some pain, weakness, and effort, I bent over and picked up my dress from the floor. I gasped at the feel of hands on my hips, pulling me. A groan left him as he ground against me.

"Don't show off your pussy if you don't want my cock. It just makes me want you more."

I could feel him hardening behind me. "Did you swallow a bottle of Viagra or something?"

"You are the drug. No other stimulants necessary." He thrusted his hips, groaning. "Love watching this ass."

I straightened, much to both of our disappointments, but it didn't keep his hands from wandering around my body. One hand was on a breast while the other slipped between my legs.

"Atticus," I whimpered.

"Fuck, I love the way you say my name like that."

I leaned my head back on his shoulder. "I should get going."

"Should?"

"It's already the afternoon." Well, only by a few minutes.

He dipped his fingers inside me before lifting them to my lips. I opened, taking them in and tasting myself as I licked his fingers clean.

"You are perfection," he whispered into my ear before stepping away, leaving me wobbling a bit. "Let me get you a car."

I pulled my dress up and reached back to tie the top. "It's okay. I can take the train." I didn't want to wait in an attempt to avoid the awkwardness that was growing in me, but I found my thighs didn't want to cooperate, and I fell into a nearby chair.

Atticus chuckled as he picked up his phone. "I do believe I promised to fuck you so hard you wouldn't be able to walk."

He had, and oh, how I thought he was just another asshole talking big. No, he delivered on his promise, and I felt it *everywhere.*

"Okay, so maybe I wouldn't be opposed to a taxi."

"I think I can do better than one of those cesspools."

I blinked at him. What other option was there?

"There is a car waiting for you out front whenever you're ready," he said a moment later. "I can't convince you to stay, can I?"

I shook my head. "Sorry. I have to work tonight."

He pulled me against his chest, his arms holding me close. "Thank you for a wonderful evening," Atticus said as he placed a kiss to my cheek, then to my lips.

"Thank you for a very memorable birthday. It's definitely one I will never forget," I admitted. It wasn't a night I believed could be topped.

"I never did ask how old you turned."

"Twenty-six."

"Hmm."

"Hmm, what?" I asked, unsure if the sound was good or bad.

A small smile graced his lips as he brushed my hair back. "Best night of my life spent with a woman nearly ten years younger than me. Unexpected."

"Best night?" I asked.

He nodded. "It was truly a pleasure meeting you."

"You too."

"Would it be presumptuous of me to assume you had a good enough time that you would be willing to see me again?"

I bit down on my bottom lip and smiled as I nodded. "I'd like that very much."

He pressed his lips to mine for a last searing kiss before I headed down to the lobby.

I was blissed out as I sat in the back of the black sedan

Atticus sent me home in. It really had been the best night of my life, and I couldn't keep the smile from my face the entire journey home.

A few days had passed, and I hadn't heard from Atticus. I couldn't deny part of me was saddened by this, but judging based on his suit and the expensive penthouse hotel room, he was bound to be a busy man.

At least, that was the reasoning I gave myself to lessen the ache in my chest.

Once, I saw a man I thought was him, but when he turned to face me, I was wrong. The bad part was the utter embarrassment of calling out his name, only to be proven wrong.

To keep my mind off him, I dove into work. I hadn't been at 130 Degrees for very long, just under two months, but I enjoyed the atmosphere of the high-end steakhouse. One meal for a couple cost a bare minimum of two-hundred dollars, and the tips were just as good.

"Ophelia," my manager, Mitchell, called out and waved me over.

"What's up, boss?"

He led us to his office and closed the door. The action had my stomach suddenly in knots because that was a "you're being fired" kind of move.

"We have a large business meeting coming in tomorrow. Our investors will be there."

"Okay."

"I want you to take the lead."

I blinked at him, happy for the opposite of my worst thoughts. "Me? What about Chris or Megan? They've been here a lot longer. I'm still learning."

Not that I didn't appreciate it, but I was still the new girl.

"They're good, but you have the best rapport with the clients. They like you. I need your personality to shine and show these men why a plate here is so expensive."

"My smile doesn't tack on an extra hundred to the bill."

He chuckled. "No, but you are great at flavor pairing and making sure everything is perfect."

"Thank you. Really, thank you."

He grinned at me. "Tomorrow won't be easy, but you'll have help. Make me proud."

"I will. I promise."

The next morning, I made certain that the large banquet table was impeccably set.

My stomach twisted in anticipation as I readied everything. I wanted to make a good impression for both myself and the restaurant. It would be my first larger party, and I would have Drake around as a helper. He was a little bit squirrelly but friendly.

"Ophelia, they're here," Mitchell called as he stuck his head into the kitchen.

I stared up at him and nodded. My nerves kicked in, and I blew out a breath before heading out onto the floor.

The atmosphere at the table screamed money and power, and as I scanned the faces, I tried to guess their drinks. When

I got to the head of the table, my mouth dropped open. He hadn't looked up, but it had only been a few days, and there was no way I would forget.

Sitting at the head of the table was none other than my one-night stand, looking devilishly handsome. When our eyes met, I caught the flash of recognition before it was covered by a look of disgust.

What is that?

I swallowed back the pain of disappointment it caused, realizing he was never going to call me, and plastered on a fake smile to cover my breaking heart. It was a stupid reaction, but I really thought we had a connection.

I was apparently the only one feeling that way. It was obvious he was out of my league, but I couldn't help but wonder. All of that was out the door, and I had to push that night from my mind. Pry my feelings away from the overwhelming sadness that came from one look as I tried to forget the best night of my life.

"Good day, gentlemen. My name is Ophelia, and I am at your service today."

NOW

ATTICUS

My grandfather is dead.

Four words I'd said to myself over and over, yet the response inside me was the same each time. There was no anguish in my emotions and little sadness in general. It was more of a relief than anything.

He was never a loving man, and I respected him, but I never loved him. Hard and harsh in every way, he'd made my life hell.

He shaped me into the man I'd become.

"Are you coming?" my brother, Hamilton, asked as I stood outside the dining room.

"I'd rather not." Nothing good was going to come from going in there.

"It's the reading of his will, and we all have to be present. Please don't torture me today by drawing it out."

I sighed before following him into the overcrowded dining room. Everyone was cloaked in black, but few mourned him. The greedy ones just wanted to know what he left them, while I was fairly certain I didn't want to hear what the old man's last jab at me would be.

All twenty of the table's chairs were taken. At the head of the table sat my father, and at the other head was the family lawyer, Alexander Corwin, with what I assumed were others from his firm to assist.

I stood against the wall next to Hamilton, with my cousin, Will, on my other side. The walls were lined with de Loughreys eagerly awaiting their take, and the gallery balcony that overlooked from the second floor was also stuffed with bodies.

"Is everyone here?" Alexander asked as he glanced around the room.

By the thickness of the legal binder in front of him, this was going to take forever, especially with a room of over seventy people.

"We are here today for the reading of the last will and testament of Atticus Charles de Loughrey."

To his brothers, my great uncles, he left money and personal items.

Unsurprisingly, money, stocks, and property, as well as a few personal items, were granted to his children—my father, Uncle Henry, Aunt Katherine, and Uncle Hugh.

Then came my turn as I was the oldest of my generation.

"To my grandson, Atticus William de Loughrey, I leave Stronghold." Alexander paused and looked around. "This residence," he added for clarification before continuing, "The position as the newest head of the de Loughrey family. He will also take over the position of CEO of de Loughrey Corporation, and with that he will inherit all my shares in the de Loughrey Corporation on his fortieth birthday."

My eyes narrowed. Why would he make me the largest shareholder?

I wasn't the only one wondering as multiple sets of eyes flickered to me. There was a catch. I just knew it.

I already knew of the impending promotion to de Loughrey family leader, patriarch of all, and that was the only non-surprise. With my father retiring, albeit slowly, the crown fell to me. There was an almost palpable shift in the air—a shift of respect and compliance.

It was the day I would be crowned.

"I apologize, Atticus. I realize you are already the CEO. This will is two years old."

"It's fine, Alexander."

"There's more."

Of course there is.

"In order to receive his shares, Stronghold, and to retain his position as CEO and head, there are two conditions which must be met. Atticus Charles has put it all into a trust with springing interest, meaning Atticus William will only gain rights to the property and shares upon fulfillment of the terms. The terms are henceforth set: If Atticus is not married upon my death, he has one year to be married or forfeit all. He also must produce an heir before his fortieth birthday. Both conditions must be met by the dates specified or he will not receive anything. If he fails to meet the requirements, the items stated will be handed to my second grandson, Rhys Geoffrey de Loughrey, whereby the same requirements will be enacted. And so on, through each male heir, until the conditions are met."

Fuck.

Fuck, fuck, fuck.

The old man got his last dig in hard.

"Comply, or lose everything I've primed you for." I could even hear the words in his voice, feel his steely gaze pinned on me.

He never liked that out of more than a dozen grandchildren, none of us were married except Elizabeth. However, he no longer considered her a de Loughrey as she was not a man and no longer held our family name. Always underestimating Elizabeth and women in general.

By the time my father had reached my age, he had multiple children already. The same for my uncles and aunt. Therefore, my grandfather believed we all should have children.

Well played, Grandfather.

I was also left with a few million dollars and some artwork. Much more money and property was given out, divided up among my siblings and cousins, and a trust was set up for eleven de Loughrey homes around the globe. It was only the tip of the iceberg, as the family owned much more than that. They were the oldest of the properties, which was why it was curious he left me Stronghold. It had been in our family since my great-great-grandfather. The original show of de Loughrey wealth to rival Vanderbilt's riches. In my eyes, it should have been the crowning property of the trust.

With every few minutes of speaking, Alexander had to take a sip of water, and by the end of hour two, his voice had become hoarse. When he finished, an elaborate symphony of paperwork was danced across the room by his assistants.

With a swipe of the pen, I accepted everything including my role, my status, and the stipulations he enacted.

I was the new ruler.

King of the de Loughreys.

"He got the final word, as usual," Hamilton said beside me as the assistant handed me my copy.

There was still more paperwork to take care of, but that would wait for another time.

"It shouldn't shock me, but I find I am surprised."

When Alexander stood, the room began to disperse, some heading home, some chatting as they awaited dinner.

As family passed I received nods and acknowledgments, as well as handshakes. However, not everyone was happy about the new power structure or distribution of my grandfather's excessive wealth.

"This isn't fair. Atticus got so much," Daniel said, making me pause.

I turned to him. "He was your great uncle. Why would he leave you more than his firstborn grandson and successor?"

He startled, not realizing I was right there. Daniel, who at twenty-five, had little pressure on him and epitomized the stereotype of families like ours by acting like a spoiled brat.

"I—"

I leaned forward, the movement cutting him off. "Isn't there a stipulation in your trust that you must maintain a job?"

"Y-yes."

Weak. So weak it made me burn with rage.

I leaned in closer to make sure he could see the displeasure in my expression and the flames behind my eyes. "Then be happy you were even here. Shut up and get out before I fire you."

His eyes widened. Pathetic. Where did this weak blood come from?

"You can't fire me."

I quirked a brow at him. Was he talking back? A low chuckle left me, and I snarled at him, "Try me."

I watched the bob of his Adam's apple as the color drained from his face. He bowed his head in submission. "I'm sorry, Atticus."

Every so often, one of the spoiled ones thought they were tough. Thought they were more than they were. Examples were made to help keep all the egos in check, and my rule had just found its first target.

Start hard to keep the insubordination down. What was asked of them all was trivial. Behave. Yet it amazed me how often someone stepped out of line.

Daniel scurried away with Petra and Phillip, thankfully heading toward the front door.

Once gone from my sight, I pulled out my phone and in one short message to cut Daniel's accounts off. The move was temporary, but his hysteria when he found he had no money would straighten out his attitude.

"Atticus," my father called.

I stuffed my phone back in my pocket and looked up. The smile on his lips coupled with the manic energy emanating from his gaze had me grinding my teeth. It hadn't been five minutes, and he was already up to something.

"Don't worry, I've got a perfect wife for you," he said as he stopped in front of me.

"Excuse me?"

"An arranged marriage. There is a girl—"

"Stop," I said, interrupting him. "Say nothing more." How many times had we had the same argument over the last decade?

His gaze hardened. "Don't be difficult, Atticus. A marriage to an influential family is a perfect solution."

"I refuse."

"Refuse?" He scoffed. "You're not really in the position to decline."

"*I* am the patriarch now. Not you," I ground out.

"How can you be a patriarch when you don't even have any children," he sneered.

"Hear me well, Father, because I will not repeat myself," I raised my voice so that all around would hear. "*I am your king.* It matters not that you are my father. I rule this family, not you. If Grandfather had died ten years ago, the responsibility would have fallen to you, but you're already entering retirement and I run the company."

"I am your *father*, and I will do what is necessary for you to succeed. You *will* marry a woman of my choosing."

"I will *never* agree to an arranged marriage, so remove that thought from your mind," I boomed out, my anger no longer tethered by a thread.

"You will come to my side of thinking."

"Stubborn old man. You need to come to my side or I will crush you."

"You're not strong enough, *son.*"

"I wouldn't challenge me."

"You have no power over me." He grinned.

There was little that I could hold over him and he knew it. Charles de Loughrey was nearly untouchable and would be a constant thorn in my side.

"Your access to the de Loughrey tower has been revoked for the next week."

His eyes widened. "What?"

It wasn't much, but my ammunition was minimal at this time. I would need to become more cunning when facing him.

"For each word you say, I will add another week. You're now at two. Your little affair with one of your assistants? As of today, she is removed."

His face was red with rage, but he somehow managed to hold himself back. My lips pulled up into a smirk.

"Bow your head before I remove your maid."

His eyes widened further.

"Oh, yes, I know about that one as well. You can't hide your indiscretions from me, Father."

His muscles were coiled right, but he managed a slight bow of his head.

"I'm glad we have reached an understanding. Now, refrain from testing me again."

I pushed past him and retrieved a drink from the bar before making my way out to the patio. I relaxed into one of the plush chairs as I swirled the amber liquid of my glass of

Bowmore 1957 whiskey while overlooking the lake. The sun gleamed across the water, giving off a calming effect in addition to the drink in my hand.

It had already begun, and that outburst was only the beginning. I could feel their eyes boring into the back of my head, hear the chattering of whispers flowing in the breeze. The weight of them settled on my shoulders, oppressive as it coiled around my chest.

The expression of my status would keep many of them in line, but during the beginning, there were going to be assholes testing me. I would make examples of them, and punishments began to form in my mind for the spoiled assholes.

The Bowmore did little to settle the stress that boiled inside. Stress that I wouldn't dare show anyone. It would be seen as weakness, an avenue of exploitation.

The new head of the family. Grandfather had lived to a ripe old age, passing at the time Father began to step back in the company. That was the only thing his stipulations didn't touch. No matter what, I was the new ruler of hundreds of de Loughreys.

The king.

My word would be the last word and law.

It was a role my grandfather and my father had shared over the last two decades, but now it was all mine.

I may not have been as heavy-handed as my father, but I would still put each and every one of them in their place with no remorse. Being the head of the family was no easy task, and while my father still held some of the familial responsibility, the bulk rested on my shoulders.

The sun sparkled across the water, turning the surface into a beautiful golden orange when a hand landed on my shoulder. The dainty yet calloused fingers told me all I needed to know.

She said nothing, though I knew she had much on her mind. After the incident, my little sister had become withdrawn. The spotlight of shame was one she vowed never to enter again. It was a time in which we'd grown closer, something our nine-year age gap had not allowed before.

Of all my siblings, Penelope was the most intuitive, and the simple weight of her hand conveyed more than anyone else could comprehend.

"They're settling for dinner," she said.

I let out a sigh as I stood, taking one last look at the lake before following her inside. The table had been extended to allow room for everyone who remained and was exquisitely set. Gold trimmed china and crystal sparkled in the richly appointed table.

All eyes fell to me as they stood, waiting, and it pleased me that none were taking that moment to test me.

The heaviness that lay upon my shoulders had my spine straightening to carry the load of all in the room as I took my place at the head of the table. Once I was seated, my father followed suit before the scooting of chairs filled the silence.

While not Shakespeare's exact words, the idiom was most apt:

Heavy is the head that wears the crown.

chapter
TWO

ATTICUS

The chatter of my family from the two-story dining room echoed in the gallery as I stared out. Small twinkling lights could be seen on the lake as fireworks boomed, sprinkling colorful bright spots against the dark sky.

The setting was familiar. I grew up in Stronghold, and now I was the lord of all I surveyed.

As long as I married.

As long as I had a child.

I knew there was no way the old man would cross over without flipping me off as he went.

The house was mine. *The* house of the de Loughrey family.

Now to find a family of my own to fill it.

That thought filled me with dread. I'd spent my life striving to be the best, to excel the business, to expand our horizons, and I was on the verge of losing it all over a fucking woman.

Lavender and linen filled my senses, and the whispered moans in the back of my mind invaded my ears. They weren't memories from either woman in whose beds I'd spent many hours. No, Bridget and Antonia were far from my thoughts. The ghostly reminder was of a woman I'd spent only one night with. A woman who tortured me weekly, and I paid her to do so.

Ophelia.

The errant thought was as mad as my behavior that evening. No, it was quite insane. The mere flash of an idea had me tilted enough I pondered if I needed to be checked out by the family physician.

Taking her home that night was one of those maneuvers I hadn't expected. Something about her beauty, the aching loneliness that almost called out to me. A siren in a sea of gyrating bodies and loud beats. Adrift with no one to save her.

Was that why I couldn't resist her? Why I continued to think of her?

"Had enough?" a familiar voice asked.

I didn't even need to look to know who it was that now leaned against the banister next to me, though I was happy to have his distraction.

"Am I that obvious?"

Rhys chuckled. "For as much as you are like Aunt Vera, you are equally like Uncle Charles."

"Except I'm not off hiding in a spare bedroom with the maid. I'm simply tired of the inane babbling."

"Are you hiding with the butler?"

I turned and narrowed my gaze on my cousin. We were

the oldest of the generation, born from the oldest of the pre-vious generation, and saddled with responsibilities that posi-tion of birth hoisted upon us.

"Simply because I'm not out fucking every slut at what-ever high-end club you are currently playing at does not mean anything. My sex life is none of your concern."

"Well, it should be yours."

"Why?"

He arched a dark brow at me. "You don't have a girlfriend."

"When the fuck do I have time for something like that?"

He held up a hand. It was a conversation we'd both had, and been given, multiple times. I was tired of the constant bar-rage about my love life, and more than once, about the threat of an arranged marriage.

Unfortunately, all that had come to a head.

"You heard the will, same as me. The family demands an heir."

"And where is your contribution?" I asked. Rhys gave me one of his sly smirks that only devils wore. "Besides, my father seems happy to continue supplying heirs."

"They are not legitimate."

"You should know," I scoffed. Being the lethal lawyer of the company, Rhys was the one who drew up all the contracts and non-disclosure agreements for my father's philandering. Those types were not entrusted to Alexander, the family law-yer. He made certain they were ironclad and that there was no way the mother or child could ever try to extort or expose the dirty laundry.

The consequences for even the slightest infraction were dealt with swiftly.

"At this rate, our mess of siblings will have families before us, and therefore, the company."

I let out a dark chuckle. "Elizabeth has already beaten us there, and the rest of my siblings? It'll be a cold day in hell before any of them settle down. I honestly think next up will be Georgiana."

"My debutante little sister?" he asked, then seemed to ponder. "She is the second youngest of our two families, but also the purest."

"I wouldn't be surprised if she was a virgin."

He shook his head. "She lost that long ago, but I will say I don't think there have been very many suitors in her bed."

"Unlike Genevieve." The youngest of our two families was also the most unruly. She failed to fall into line and proved to be difficult to rein in.

"Genevieve is just lashing out, and you know this."

"Perhaps, but she is the biggest thorn in my side. Now this? Grandfather sure got the last laugh in."

"You expected anything less?"

"The fireworks are an odd touch."

A harsh laugh left him before he took a sip. "It's him spitting from the depths of hell."

I scoffed at that as the red sparkles glittered against the dark sky.

"Why not ask one of your playthings to fill the role?" he asked.

"Are you actually pushing marriage on me?"

"If not, you know it will move to me, and I won't be able to fulfill the requirements. It will then move to Hamilton, and if he fails, down to Silas and Atlas. I don't want the family legacy falling to ruin."

"Such faith you have in your brothers."

A sigh left him. "It's not that, and you know it. Silas…I do hate seeing him when he's…off."

"He needs to fucking find a way to keep himself calm."

"Atlas is trying. He's the only one who can get through to Silas."

The twins were brilliant when they worked together. However, in recent years Silas had been exhibiting the darker side of being a de Loughrey.

"Elizabeth would make a fine CEO."

"A woman as CEO?" Rhys's eyes widened as he looked out the window. "Look, see? There is Grandfather spewing his displeasure."

Another round of fireworks boomed.

"He's gone. We can surely change things."

"Elizabeth is the only one fit to be an executive."

"What about your sister?"

He paused and I realized I'd unwittingly hit Rhys's landmine. He quickly downed the rest of his drink and shook his head. "Georgiana is too sweet. Some days I wonder if she's a de Loughrey at all."

Crisis averted. "She's just found her niche. A way to stand out."

"Much like Genevieve, and how could we forget the Tainted Princess?"

A groan left me. "This is a problem. What am I going to do?"

He sighed. "I don't know, but whatever it is, you need to figure it out soon, or you will have no choice but to go with an arranged marriage."

My jaw clenched. "Never. If I am forced to spend my life with a woman, it will be one of my choosing, not an obligation."

He clapped his hand on my shoulder. "Start hunting."

Memories of that night flooded in again. The way she moved beneath me. The need that kept me going longer and harder than ever before.

Look at me.

Look at me… What the fuck was I thinking?

Sex was a vehicle to blow off steam, but that night I needed more. Three words that had me pleading for something I had never desired. A look into her soul as I made her come undone.

An act that had me unable to forget her.

chapter
THREE

OPHELIA

A sigh left me as I stood in line, waiting to pay for yet another pair of black pants and a white button-down shirt. That was the problem with working at a high-end restaurant—the smallest amount of fading, staining, or holes of any kind, and they had to be replaced. I'd seen more than one employee sent home because of it.

I never imagined I would spend more on work clothes than I did on regular clothes, but then again, I didn't care if my everyday wares were faded or ripped or stained. Okay, I did a little, but how many pairs of jeans with blown out knees did I have? Or tees with holes that I wore until the hole was too big, and often I still would just throw a tank on underneath?

The restaurant where I worked, 130 Degrees, was a place I could never even imagine eating at and was lucky for the few scraps of leftovers I did get.

"Ophelia?" a familiar voice called.

I turned and my stomach dropped, but I put on my best smile. "Jennifer, hi. How are you?"

Once upon a time, we were roommates in college, and friends.

She hadn't changed a bit. Perfectly styled brunette waves, chocolate-brown eyes, and the posture and style of a woman who thought she was better than everyone else.

That had never been something I noticed until I left my pharmaceutical sales position. I didn't even last a year before I left. It wasn't for me, despite the money. When I became a waitress to pay the bills, I was suddenly beneath her.

"Wonderful. How are you?"

"Good."

"What are you up to these days? Still waiting tables?"

"Um, actually, I am. I work at 130 Degrees."

Her eyes widened. "Really? My fiancé and I—oh, yeah, Luthor and I got engaged!" She threw her hand out and nearly smacked me in the face with a huge assortment of diamonds.

"That's great!" I said, calling up all the fake enthusiasm I could. "Such a beautiful ring." Tacky was more like it. Cluster rings could be beautiful, but the one she was wearing was a no for me.

"Isn't it? It's three carats total." She tilted her hand back to look at it. "Anyway, we were looking at venues for our engagement party. Does 130 Degrees have a room or anything that we could hold it in?"

"How many people?" I asked.

"About fifteen. Maybe you could get a discount for a friend." She grinned.

"I think the base rate for an event like that is about two hundred and fifty dollars a head, plus any alcohol."

I took a little bit of sick pleasure watching the way her eyes bulged.

"Two-fifty a person? That's outrageous."

I shrugged. "I have one customer who comes in every week. His bill is always almost two hundred just for lunch."

"Well, I'll have to see what Luthor thinks."

I gave her the biggest, fakest smile I could. "Sure thing. If you decide to, just drop by and talk to the manager, Mitchell."

"Who comes in every week for a lunch like that?" she asked.

I knew the curiosity would get to her. The past few years had taught me that some people only cared about status symbols and money. While those were nice things to have, especially the money, there was more to life.

I was also certain that if she ever met Atticus, he would send her running out the door crying in less than five minutes. I'd seen him do it before to some high-society blonde trying to sit with him.

"Just some guy I know." By not sharing his name and coming across as having a casual relationship with a mysterious, rich guy would just eat her up. I knew her well enough that status and material things meant more to her than people.

When did I become so catty? Oh, right, when I couldn't be her friend because I was a mere waitress.

"Well, maybe I'll have to come by to meet Mr. Mysterious."

"Sure." I smiled, deciding not to tell her it was reservation only.

Unless you were Atticus or some other major money player.

"It was so good to see you again, Ophelia," she said.

I waved. "Bye."

My expression fell, and I rolled my eyes. She was just too stuck up for me to handle.

I started when I found the employee running the cash register staring, wide-eyed.

"Wasn't that Luthor Anderson's fiancée?"

I sighed as I threw my items up onto the counter. "Yup." Of course, she would be recognized. Luthor, after all, was one of baseball's most shocking trades. A center fielder that just signed a three-year, twenty-million-dollar contract with the Yankees, which was why I was surprised by the ring on her finger and her balking at the price at 130 Degrees. Maybe he had her on a tight financial leash.

Then again, we were in Manhattan.

After a stop at the grocery, a train transfer, and a bus transfer, I was finally home. It seemed like half my day was spent commuting into and out of Manhattan, but there wasn't much I could do about it. The tips I made at 130 Degrees couldn't compare to anything near me, and until I figured out what I wanted to do with my life, I was stuck with the horrid routine.

I shuffled into my studio apartment and dropped my bags of clothes on the ground before moving to the kitchen. I pulled at the refrigerator door handle and cursed when it slammed into the oven and bounced back shut.

"Shit."

I opened the door a little more gently and slid the half-gallon of milk and sandwich fixings in, then let it close. The counter was already cluttered, but by counter, I meant the six inches that surrounded the sink. It was a joke of a kitchen, but so were rent prices.

As much as it sucked, I really couldn't complain much. At least I wasn't still living with my mom and my stepdad, Lou. From the moment he came into my life, I disliked him. He brought out the worst in my mother. They were shit parents to the two girls they had together. I hated to leave Brooke and Andrea with them, but I had to get away from being afraid of a man who would smack me for the simple fact that I wasn't his child. That my mother dared have a child before he met her.

Away from the mother who blamed me for "provoking" him.

I was out of there the second I graduated from high school. I spent the summer on friends' couches while I worked, and then when college started, I lived in the dorms. Thankfully, I was able to stay there over the summer as well, giving me no reason to return home.

By the time I graduated, I was over three hundred thousand dollars in debt.

For undergrad.

It was unreal.

Thankfully, I was able to get a well-paying job right out of school, making a hundred grand my first year. I had a decent apartment, could go out with friends like Jennifer, save for the first time in my life, and live a decent, miserable life.

It didn't take long to realize I didn't have the personality for it. I hated being a pharmaceutical sales representative. I hated being the salesperson pushing something I wasn't even entirely sure I could agree with, let alone put into my body.

I also didn't care for the person I was becoming. Being that kind of salesperson colored my soul.

After eleven months and four days, I quit. Gave up my great apartment and moved into a cheaper place back in my old neighborhood.

I liked the lab work of biology and chemistry, the science side of my degree, but I applied to dozens of clinical lab technician positions in various fields that never led to any offers. In all that, I found I could use my knowledge with food, which was the beginning of my matching and pairing of different items.

The chef at 130 Degrees was great in working with me, and I helped him sculpt a few of the restaurant's signature items. It was something I enjoyed, but it wasn't a job.

Despite my meager living, I was happier than when I worked as a sales rep. Still, I was constantly applying to jobs that interested me.

Even if I didn't have any real friends, just a few people I occasionally did things with, and I only went on the occasional date, it was better. I was a loner as it was. I always had been. It wasn't like Lou would allow me to have friends over, and whatever Lou wanted, Mom went along with.

My loner status was how I ended up alone on my birthday

last year, and somehow it ended up being the best birthday I'd ever had in my life. It was all due to one man.

Too bad one night didn't turn into more, but I found that Atticus in the light of day wasn't the man I spent the night in bed with.

Nearly a year later, he still haunted me. Every single week, there he was, looking as handsome as ever. Every week, those blue eyes met mine, and I got a hint of that man I met.

He was reserved and demanding; everything had to be perfect. The man had no problem complaining about the smallest thing, though it had been a few months now since my name had rolled off his tongue with the dark undercurrent that made my stomach clench in all the wrong ways.

Instead, it was those hollow eyes. Not empty, but there was something complicated in their depths. A heaviness I couldn't figure out. His dark blond brows were always crinkled in a permanent scowl, lips in a perfect Cupid's bow, straight nose, defined cheekbones, jaw clenched creating a hard line sometimes sprinkled with a light scruff, all topped with a perfectly styled head of dark blond hair.

Then there was the suit that looked like it was molded to his form, and I knew he was hiding the body of a god beneath the layers. I'd seen it. Touched it. Been with it intimately.

And down the rabbit hole I went.

That was what happened when I started thinking about Atticus. It always led to remembering his lips against mine, his body covering me as he thrust inside. An Adonis that drew me in with the promise of pleasure.

It didn't help that I hadn't been with a man since then,

leaving me with nothing but a memory that no man would ever be able to compete with.

Did he ever think of me?

It was kind of a hopeless, wistful longing for a man who had the last forty-some weeks to ask me out and hadn't even hinted that he even remembered that night. He didn't crave me the way I craved him.

Well, I craved his body. His personality could use some improvement. But I supposed that was what duct tape was for.

Even then, there was something about my mysterious Atticus that drew me in, kept me thinking about him, against my better judgment.

My constant tormentor.

chapter
FOUR

ATTICUS

My teeth mashed together as I stared at the screen. Ever since the will reading, my world had been a shitshow. Whiny siblings and cousins, even aunts and uncles, all coming to me to complain that my grandfather didn't leave them more.

As if they wanted for anything.

Then there was the incessant badgering about marriage. I'd begun to lock myself away at every opportunity, hiding from relatives, which was difficult when you worked in a building with over thirty other de Loughreys, each one knowing exactly where your office was.

"Mr. de Loughrey?" my assistant called from the doorway.

"What?" I snapped, not even looking her way. I knew Holly wouldn't be affronted by my attitude. She'd dealt with it for years, but she also knew me in ways many didn't.

"Your father is on his way."

"Fuck," I hissed. My father was supposed to be retiring, but the old man couldn't keep his controlling hands out of the company. It was my turn to rule, but every time he came into my office and chided me on the way I was handling things, I felt like a little boy being scolded.

He stepped back after the fourth scandal. Not that it affected the family or the company. That wasn't something Charles de Loughrey would ever allow.

However, that did mean that I rose as the new head of the family, the ruler of numerous fuckups, stuck-up socialite bitches, and family that would sooner cut my throat to gain leverage than help me in any way. He was there to add to the drama.

"Atticus, my boy," my father's boisterous voice boomed as he entered. Charles loved an audience and to be the center of attention, and his expression fell when he saw the empty chairs—I was alone.

"Father. What brings you here?" I asked with a forced smile.

"Nothing. I was bored and wanted to see how things were going."

Lies. He saw the drop in the stock market, and I knew the will decree was going to come up. There was also the arranged marriage business that had me avoiding him as much as possible.

"The company is doing fine. The setback was due to the economy and not the company. Or did you fail to notice the dip in all stocks?"

"I did. That isn't the only reason I came to see you today. I wanted to talk to you about a personal matter."

Personal matter? Fuck me. What did the old man do now?

"Just give Holly her name and address along with the amount on your way out." I turned my attention to the phone that was buzzing on my desk.

Hamilton.

I could use him as an excuse. "I should take—"

"You're almost thirty-six," he said, pulling my attention back from my escape route. "You're closing in on the forty mark. That isn't much time to find a woman to bear a child. Not to mention you have only eleven months to marry."

"I still have time. Besides, you were still fathering into your forties. And should I even mention your fifties and sixties?"

His gaze narrowed, and that explosive anger simmered beneath the surface. "Watch your tongue."

"Then fucking keep it in your pants. You're too old to be knocking up the maids or whatever pretty young thing catches your eye. I'm tired of writing checks to pay the women off."

Somewhere in the world, there were children who had no clue the identity of their father. At least one was younger than Elizabeth's little girl, Madeline.

And they would never know. Some of the women chose to terminate their pregnancy after getting their hush money, but there were at least two alive and growing.

Never knowing what a fucking bastard their father was. At least they were saved that.

"It's your duty to clean up the mess now. You're the leader."

"Then how about fucking your wife? Or has it been so

long you don't even know how to engage in conversation with the woman you've shared a bed with for forty years?"

"Vera is aware of what she married for, and it wasn't my fidelity."

Another statement that alluded to the possibility of more half-siblings somewhere in the world and closer to my age. Fucking philandering asshole.

"And you will do the same."

"The hell I will." Two weeks ago, I told him there was no way in hell I was agreeing to an arranged marriage. Now he stood in front of me trying again, but with more malice and dominance in his tone to bully me into acquiescing. He should have known by now that wouldn't work on me. I was not so weak to bend to his demands.

"I have the perfect girl lined up," he pressed.

"Don't," I ground out. Fucking thick skull refused to accept my decision.

"Amelia Harris, of Harris Hotels."

A fucking socialite? Hell, no.

The name surprised me. A third-generation hotel heiress. Something worse than what I normally encountered—gold-digging, social-ladder-climbing, self-absorbed bitches. At least the latter would suck my cock like my cum was one-hundred-dollar bills in order to get something.

I'd dealt with that enough with my family, and I didn't want it sleeping next to me in bed.

There was a reason I didn't date. A reason I had acquaintances with benefits. They sure as fuck weren't my friends.

"No," I ground out.

"It would be a great partnership and acquisition for the company."

"I told you. I will not do an arranged marriage. Ever. I thought I was quite clear on the matter."

"You will do it if you wish to remain CEO."

I rounded my desk to stand in front of him. To make him bow to *my* authority, *my* dominance. "Listen here and listen good—I refuse to take part in any arranged marriage. Stop. I have grown this company more in the last five years than you did in the twenty before."

"Your ruthless brother had a lot to do with that."

"Perhaps, but I initiated the deals. I'm not about to marry some soulless bitch who I can't even get hard for. You want an heir, I'll give you one, but I'll choose the woman."

His expression never wavered. "She'll be joining us for dinner soon."

Our eyes were locked, neither backing down. "Have fun."

"You will be there."

"Or what? I'm not a child anymore."

"But you are *my* child, Atticus. And you will remain in control of this company by any means necessary, including taking on an arranged marriage."

Ah, that was what it was about. Pride. He simply couldn't handle seeing the company fall into the hands of anyone other than his progeny.

I stepped back around my desk. "I will choose my own wife, and it won't be a marriage of obligation."

A harsh laugh sprang from his lips. "I can't wait to meet her, this unicorn you expect to find and engage in that stupid emotion called love and marry all in less than a year. When that fails, I will be here to pull your ungrateful ass from the fire, and you *will* take Amelia's hand."

With that, he left.

Every muscle in me was tense, coiled tight. I needed a release, and thus the phone sitting on my desk became a casualty of my anger when I grabbed it and slammed it against the far wall with a roar.

I was breathing heavily, anger rolling through me as I stared at the carnage of bent and broken plastic that lay scattered across the carpet.

Familia ante omnia. Growing up, I just thought it was referencing to family loyalty. That was not our family's interpretation.

Family above all. Family above your own wants and desires.

An arranged marriage was the source of many of the de Loughrey family's issues, at least within the ruling branch. Everything from cheating to children born of affairs and portraying the perfect image without the ability to understand what a functioning relationship was supposed to look like—and that was just the surface.

The younger ones were rebellious, the leash around their necks looser as attention drifted. Genevieve, my youngest sister, was a constant thorn in my side, and Penelope's strong will to be her own person was an ongoing battle because of the microscope we were always under. Gen's antics often took the pressure off other family members, like the twins. More precisely, Silas.

What I needed was more than a mere wife. More than

someone to drain my cock. It was there, sitting just on the edge of my thoughts. What I wanted. What I *needed.*

A knock sounded, pulling my attention from the wreckage. "Come in."

"Everything okay, boss?" Holly asked, closing the door behind her.

"I hate him."

She pursed her lips and moved to stand in front of me. "Going to tell me?"

I blew out a breath. "Why are you my assistant?"

She shrugged. "Because I like annoying you."

"But you don't."

She blew out a breath. "Look, Att, you're my friend," she began, using the nickname I despised. "I know we have this whole boss-employee relationship tangled in there as well, but I care about you. I've put up with the whole stick-up-your-ass de Loughrey attitude for eighteen years. Pretty sure I'm the only one who can wrangle you in."

"While I'm pretty sure you're my only true friend."

She smiled and patted my cheek. "Yup. And that's why you keep me around even when I forget to order you lunch."

A chuckle left me, and I shook my head. "You get by because you're the only one who can lighten my moods."

"The curse of the gifted."

The skyline held my attention as the conversation with my father played on repeat. He wasn't one to make baseless threats. That wasn't the Charles de Loughrey way. That inkling of an idea, the stir of possibility, came back to life.

The only alternative.

I let my guard down with her more than I had with any-one in my life.

"I'm about to do something truly brilliant or epically stupid."

"I've got the parachutes packed."

"Call Jack for me, have him set up an in-house sampling of the largest diamond rings in the city as soon as possible. Nothing less than a six-carat center stone." Normally I talked with my personal assistant myself, but he and Holly had developed a great working partnership, often taking care of things without my knowledge. A good thing, as trivial matters only served to piss me off since I had little time to deal with them. For four years, Jack had been the model assistant. He perfectly handled the blend of organizing my life outside the office and rarely being seen.

She blew out a breath. "Oh, we're jumping now."

"I have just over eleven months to get married. Time is ticking."

She nodded. "I'll find a space in your schedule in the next two days. What are you going to do?"

"What else does one do when setting up a business arrangement?"

A smile lit up her face. "You see the Lethal Lawyer."

I gave her a curt nod, and she headed out the door.

For half of my life, Holly had stood beside me. Without her friendship to calm my ire, I had little doubt I would have ended up a version of my father. Perhaps Hamilton and I would have been closer, seeing as he was much like him.

I checked my calendar, then Rhys's, looking for a good

time to talk. Through pure luck, we were both free, at least meeting-wise, and it seemed the best opportunity to pull him in on my plan.

"I'll be back," I said to Holly, who nodded as I headed toward the elevators. "Atticus!" Hamilton called out, stopping me in my tracks.

It wasn't that I'd been avoiding my younger brother, simply that I'd been avoiding everyone, and that was why it took great strength to turn into his office, shutting the door behind me.

As soon as I was seated, his grey eyes were narrowed at me.

"Why do I have a meeting scheduled with Harris Hotels?" Hamilton asked.

I blew out a breath. "Because our father is a conniving asshole."

Hamilton let out a groan, his jaw clenching as his hands flexed. "He wants us all to dance to his tune."

"Yes."

"I know we haven't talked much since the will reading. What are you going to do?"

"That's a question I've been asking myself for the last few weeks. If you were in my position, what would you do?" Curiosity gnawed at me. Even though he was ruthless like our father, Hamilton also hated the idea of arranged marriages.

Honestly, I wasn't sure he would ever marry because he hated infidelity just as much.

"Tell him to fuck off, look at my little black book, and figure out who I wanted to be wrapped around my dick for the next however many years. My advice? You already have

Bridget and Antonia. Figure out which one you want to put a ring on and be done."

Bridget and Antonia.

Hamilton wasn't the first to mention the women I'd casually dated and fucked for years. No strings, just my dates for events and to warm my cock when I desired. They were used to the high-profile life, and they weren't interested in me solely for money. The problem was that every single time I thought about them, tried to decide which one, those fucking brown eyes covered my vision.

Look at me.

"Mother has already started planning your wedding."

I quirked a brow. "Has she?"

He nodded. "Elizabeth told me."

"Wonderful," I ground out.

"Atticus…pick someone soon. I'll stall this meeting, push it out as far as I can, but I can't hold Harris off forever. Father will stick his nose into things, and you know he will start the merger process without our consent."

"I'm the fucking CEO. Hell, you are second."

"I'm well aware. You don't have to remind me. What you have to do is ask someone, anyone, to marry you and bring them to the family dinner."

I shook my head. "He won't stop there."

"No, he won't. But make sure whomever you pick can't be bought by him."

The words were like ice to my veins. I wouldn't put it past our father to do something to thwart my desires. Familia ante omnia, after all.

After leaving Hamilton's office, I moved down a few floors to the legal department. Rhys's office was on the west side of the building with a view of the Hudson.

A little scrap of a woman stopped in front of me, her eyes wide, binders clutched tightly to her chest. With a squeak, she did a sudden snap to the left and raced away.

I stared after her in confusion before stopping at Rhys's assistant's desk. The brunette stared at her computer, blinking, with her lips parted almost in horror. There was a frozen quality about her.

Rhys had a high turnover in assistants for reasons I hadn't figured out, but I didn't care either. It was, however, annoying when I arrived and the girl sitting at the desk outside his office didn't even have a nameplate, leaving me standing there attempting to get her attention.

I cleared my throat, and her pale, fear-filled expression turned to me.

"Is he in?"

She nodded, then her brow furrowed like she was trying to figure out what to do next.

"First day?"

"Y-yes," she squeaked out.

She looked up at me with hope in her eyes that I might tell her it was all right, that she was doing well, or some shit I'd witnessed Holly do time and time again. Instead, I stared at her, wondering if she was going to make it through the day.

"If you're this flustered on day one, you should probably quit." All hope faded from her face, and her eyes began to water.

"Atticus, are you terrorizing the help again?" Rhys called, and I turned my attention to the now-open door.

"Hmph, if I remember, you were the one who used a fire-cracker to blow up the breakfast cart, which would make *you* the help terrorist." I stepped inside and closed the door, then settled into the plush chair across from his desk.

"Margie wouldn't come near me for years," he chuckled. "What brings you down from your perch?"

"I need a couple of contracts drawn up."

"Just send the information to Jennifer, or Jessica…what is her name?" Rhys said as he looked toward the door, then shrugged.

"It's not business. It's personal."

His brow quirked as he looked at me and leaned back in his chair. "I'm listening."

Not going to Alexander meant top secret, and Rhys loved to know all the dirty secrets to use for his advantage at a later date.

I pulled a folded-up piece of paper from my inner jacket pocket and held it out. Rhys's eyes studied me as he pulled it from my grasp and unfolded it. His forehead creased as he scanned it.

"Really, cousin?"

"Shred it when you're done."

He sighed. "I'll have a preliminary draft for you later today."

With a curt nod, I stepped out and headed back toward my office. The air on my floor was infinitely clearer. Perhaps it was due to fewer occupants on the floor, but I felt much more comfortable in my arena.

Upon rounding a corner, I bumped into a small brunette. Files dropped from her arms to the floor, exposing a glorious rack.

What was it with peons getting in my way today?

"I'm so sorry, Mr. de Loughrey. Please don't fire me," she begged as she dropped to the floor to pick everything up.

I blinked down at the small girl in front of me. Had I gained such a reputation that the poor girl trembling in front of me feared me? Was that the curse of running the de Loughrey family? I didn't know who she was, but she had been around long enough to know who I was, meaning she worked for either my father or my brother, maybe my uncle. Then again, she could have worked for me, but I didn't pay attention to any of my assistants past Holly.

"I don't understand why you think I would fire you for running into me."

I clenched my jaw, waiting for her eyes to meet mine, but became impatient when she refused. A mousy little thing, but the sight of her breasts stirred something, and I began to wonder if she'd be a perfect vehicle to relieve my pent-up frustration.

"They are two ways this can go. One, I help you gather up your files and send you back to work. The other is you following me back to my office and put those pretty pink lips…" I stopped myself. Stopped myself from divulging my desires, my need to work off some of the mounting aggression pumping through me.

She stared up at me with wide eyes, a blush blossoming on her pale cheeks. The innocent look only stoked the fire in me, awakening the wicked king all too willing to succumb to my baser needs.

I wasn't my father, and I refused to prey upon employees. The girl still staring up at me tested that resolve. I didn't like to mix business with pleasure, especially not with a young, naïve little intern, no matter how much my cock wanted it.

Instead, I glared down at her. "You shouldn't look at men like that unless you are wishing for depravity."

There was no need for a response. I simply walked away. Bridget was a brunette as well. Perhaps I'd give her a call. Ease the desire to have my cum sucked from me.

"Office. Now."

In my periphery, Holly hopped up from her chair and followed me through the door. Once she was in, I closed the door and headed over to the wet bar to pour myself a drink.

I said nothing, and Holly had been around me long enough not to ask.

"Am I really that scary?" I asked as I slammed the empty glass on the counter, then poured more before turning back to her.

"Att, you're a de Loughrey. Scary is in your blood."

I glared at her use of my nickname once again as I passed her on my way to the sofa chairs in the corner. She followed behind and took a seat across from me.

"I have high expectations."

"You also take no prisoners and have a serious case of resting bitch face."

"Seriously?"

She quirked a brow at me. "Your aura screams 'get the fuck out of my way' everywhere you go."

"It comes with the territory. I constantly feel like I'm wrangling a house full of toddlers, especially of late."

"There is a flip side to your harsh front."

I scoffed at that. "And what is that?"

"Nobody crosses you."

"Constant aggravation." The replacement phone Holly already procured and set up began ringing, but I ignored it.

"You need a vacation," she said and pulled out her phone, probably looking at my schedule.

"What's that?"

She rolled her eyes. "Time away from the office."

I shook my head and frowned. "It's not a good time." I couldn't even remember the last time I took two days off in a row.

"It's never a good time."

"Maybe it's better. Less relationships I have to manage."

"I'm just saying, sitting on a beach, drinking a mai tai would do you some good."

"Thanks, Holly."

"I've always got your back. Don't worry your pretty little head over being scary."

I glared at her. "Do you ever see me worrying about what anyone thinks of me?"

She laughed at that. "No, but I know that ego still needs fluffing from time to time."

"How is it I've never fucked you?" My phone began to

buzz in my hand, my mother's name on the screen, but I ignored it.

"You're not my type."

"I'm everyone's type." Money made the world go round and women fell to their knees in front of me with their mouths wide open.

"I'm married. To a beautiful woman."

"That just says threesome to me."

She shook her head and rolled her eyes. "Do you need me to bring out the little black book?"

It was tempting, but much more of a hassle than calling Bridget. The socialites that I'd spent a night with in the past were insipid, and I couldn't stand their constant plying to gain a hold into my life.

There was only one woman who was going to accomplish that, and that was because she wasn't even trying.

"No. I do need a lunch reservation. I need out of here for an hour or two. We'll call that my vacation." Reservation was incorrect. I never needed a reservation where I was going, but it allowed Holly to inform them I was coming and to ready it.

"Table for one?"

I nodded. "The usual. And I'm going to leave my phone with you."

She blinked at me like I'd spoken a foreign language. "Leave your phone?"

"Yes."

"Why?"

The phone went off again, and I rubbed my temples. "Five fucking minutes of peace." Something I was desperate for, especially recently, with family coming out of the woodwork: third cousins I may have encountered at a family reunion, a second cousin on my mother's side, and even closer relations who wanted to ride the high of my inheritance.

After all, if I fulfilled the terms of the will, I would become the richest and most powerful de Loughery since my grandfather. I would even surpass his reign.

She gave a curt nod. "I guess lunch without your phone would be a vacation, and you'll have Damien nearby. Still, you should fly down to Haven for the weekend. Get away from the city."

Haven, our island in the Bahamas, wasn't a bad idea. I could take one of my playthings and spend the weekend fucking everything out on her. She would love the private Bahamian island, and I could get my dick sucked out on the pool edge overlooking the pristine aqua water.

The problem was that if a single member of my family found out I was going, it would no longer just be me and my playdate.

"I'll think about it," I said as I headed out the door.

My afternoon was filled with back-to-back meetings, and I picked up the pace. The longer I was there, the more time I would have to center myself before I let loose on someone. In our five-minute conversation, the phone had rung five times, and I would snap if I didn't get away. My fuse was much shorter of late.

Being free from the shackles of my phone was settling. Each step took me further from the demands that constantly weighed me down. If there was any true emergency, Holly knew where to find me.

I stepped up to the entrance of 130 Degrees and was immediately greeted by Mitchell, the day manager.

"Good afternoon, sir. It's a pleasure seeing you again."

"Pleasantries, Mitchell?" It was a custom we had deleted from our encounters in lieu of more casual conversation.

"Sorry," he whispered as he led me back to my private booth. "We have a food critic here today, and I'm trying to make an impression.

"Wonderful to see you again, Mitchell," I replied, playing along. While 130 Degrees had been doing spectacularly well with critics, putting an exemplary perception out was a good idea.

Not that I really cared what they said, but I knew Mitchell did. He took pride in his work, and it showed.

He held the curtain back, and I slid into my booth. A sigh of relief left me when it closed, the heavy curtains dampening the sounds of the other patrons, which was aided by a small speaker playing classical remixed songs heavy on string instruments. It was a niche I completely blamed on Penelope, but I found it soothing and upbeat at the same time.

I doubted anyone who knew me would guess that.

"Good day, Atticus," my waitress said as she entered my dim sanctuary and set a brandy down in front of me.

"Ophelia," I greeted. "It may be a double today."

She nodded. "The usual? Or should I tempt you with the wagyu today?"

The usual was the healthier option, but the steak might help me get through the day. "Tempt."

"Pan-roasted fingerling potatoes with pancetta?"

"Yes."

"Broccolini?"

I nodded. "Not—"

"Charred. Yes, sir. Anything else?" she asked, meeting my gaze for the first time.

Her brown eyes were wide and met mine with respect, friendliness, and that edge of regret of missed opportunities that prevailed between us. One I was now determined to erase.

"That will be all for now."

"I will be back shortly," she said with a smile before parting the curtains and disappearing.

Ophelia had been my designated waitress at least once a week since that business meeting nearly a year ago.

I made it so.

Just so I could see her again.

I'd been having lunch at 130 Degrees for much longer than that, but not as often as when I discovered she worked here.

Before her, I'd scared more than one server out of the restaurant. Ophelia, on the other hand, caught on quickly to my habits as well as my moods. She knew me only as Atticus, as did all the staff, and the table was reserved for me and me alone.

I was certain rumors floated around about it, but the managers were told to either squash them or tell them I was an investor and it was the investors' table. The truth was—I owned it. It was a side venture of mine and run by my holding company, Aegean Rule. There were a few other businesses they managed, and all were outside the de Loughrey hold.

Not everything fell under the de Loughrey Corporation, many of us having other smaller businesses as well as charities. It was more about control than income. The money made in a year barely covered my personal staff for a few months.

Lunch wasn't my only reason for visiting 130 Degrees, but because my frequency had increased since discovering Ophelia, my presence was not out of the ordinary. However, my reason stretched beyond satiating my stomach.

It was torture every time I laid eyes on her. A desire for something I told myself I couldn't have.

When my meal was finished and after I paid the bill, I pulled out a unique business card and held it out to her.

"Come to my office. Tomorrow. Nine a.m., and don't be late."

She blinked at me, her gaze moving down to the card, then back up. "Why would I go to your office?"

I stood up and moved to stand beside her. "I need to talk to you about a private matter." There wasn't enough privacy in the restaurant to discuss my idea.

"Don't tell me you gave me something last year."

I froze and stared at her. It was the first time in a year either one of us had even alluded to that night.

I leaned in, taking note of the sweet scent of her skin. Just that small inhale calmed me in a way nothing had before. "This has nothing to do with that encounter, but if you want me to give you the same thing for your birthday I did last year, I'm more than happy to oblige." I reveled in her sharp intake of breath. "Give reception this card when you *arrive.*" My lips brushed against her neck, just below her ear.

After crossing through the doors, my blood buzzed in anticipation, making my skin feel alive. The morning could not come fast enough.

"**Y**ou have got to be fucking kidding me," I hissed as I looked from the map on my phone to the building in front of me.

The butterflies kicked up in my stomach. I couldn't be in the correct place. I just couldn't. The card Atticus had given me was black with a metallic-gold inlay that held only a symbol on one side and an address on the other. But the symbol didn't match the logo etched onto the glass.

The de Loughrey building was the third tallest in the city and was completely inhabited by the de Loughrey Corporation, one of the largest companies in the world. They were so large that de Loughrey was a household name.

All night I'd worried about why Atticus wanted to see me. It was so out of the blue and had my stomach in such terrible knots that I'd barely slept.

For the last year, waiting on him every week had been torture. The looks, the attraction; they may have been one-sided, and I hated myself for that. For letting him continue to affect me. For forcing me to follow his request instead of telling him to fuck off all with one look from his beautiful blue eyes, one brush of his shoulder against mine.

Instead, I stood in front of a symbol for one of the most powerful families in the world, wondering what the fuck I was doing there. With a deep breath I stuffed the card back in my bag and entered through the glass doors.

The elevator bays were surrounded by a large desk with security scanning identification cards as people entered. It seemed a time-consuming process, and I wondered how many people were late due to early morning lines, though it seemed to be moving at a quick pace.

There was even a line at the front desk checking guests in.

As I looked around at the sharp business suits and crisp clothing, I instantly regretted my casual attire. Black leggings, ballet flats, flowy lilac tunic, and jean jacket with my ratty messenger bag stood out, and I'd received a few dubious looks.

"Can I help you, miss?"

I blinked and stepped forward to the counter. "Um, yeah, I'm here to see…" It was then I realized I didn't even know his last name.

"The name, please."

I nodded and pulled back the flap of my bag, digging for the card I'd had in my hand moments before. "He gave me a card…" In one of the pockets, I finally located the matte black card and held it out. "He said to give you this?"

It came out more as a question, but that was because of the way he looked from the card to me, then back to the card. He gently took it from me as if it held some mystical power, turned it under the light of the scanner, then held it back out.

"Identification, please."

I blinked again before reaching into my bag for my wallet and pulling it out. I grimaced as I wrestled the card from the slot and handed it over. The stare down I was getting wasn't one of animosity but more of curiosity.

After scanning my identification, he gave it back and then held out a similar black card, which was more like a hotel key card.

He leaned forward and pointed toward a single elevator. "Go over there and scan that card. It will open and take you where you need to go."

"And where is that?"

"To Mr. de Loughrey's office. One of his assistants will be waiting for you."

I froze as I tried to decipher what he'd just said. The name weighed on me before settling in my stomach, then dropping the floor out from beneath me.

"Who did you just say?"

"Mr. Atticus de Loughrey. You better get going—he doesn't tolerate tardiness."

I gave a shaky nod while I tried to find words and managed to unintelligibly thank him as I stepped away.

De Loughrey.

Atticus was a *de Loughrey*.

For the last year that I'd known Atticus, I knew he had money. From the hotel penthouse that night to the hundreds he spent on lunch twice a week. But being a de Loughrey? I never in my life thought I would ever meet one, let alone sleep with one.

I swallowed hard, my heart hammering in my chest with each step that closed the gap between me and the looming elevator. I slipped the card into the reader, the doors immediately opened, and as I stepped into the cab, it hit me.

Oh my God, I fucked a de Loughrey!

I'd thought about that night so many times since my birthday. It was shocking when I found him sitting at the head of the table in a private dining room a week after that. The way his blue eyes widened in shock. I didn't know what to do other than to go into my greeting, and we never spoke about it. We never even hinted at it until yesterday, but I was always thinking about it.

The man I remembered was just an illusion compared to reality. At first, I thought he was just angry with a mistake I'd made, but I came to learn that he was just brash. A harsh contrast to the man I met that night.

When the elevator closed in, only slowing when it reached the top floors, did I understand. The highest floors usually correlated with the highest in the company, and the doors opened at the top.

Atticus's bad attitude came from his position. More

work and responsibility went hand-in-hand with greater stress. That didn't mean his mood was excusable, it just meant I finally got why he hid away at lunch. Why the restaurant catered to making him a sanctuary.

I wasn't even a step out of the elevator when a woman appeared in front of me. She was almost my height in heels, with sleek brown hair and warm brown eyes.

"Welcome, Miss Evans. My name is Holly, I'm Mr. de Loughrey's personal assistant."

"H-hi," I stuttered. It was all really settling in.

"Follow me," she said with a reassuring smile.

My stomach was in knots as we walked, clenching and unclenching, and as we passed the placard next to a huge wooden door, I nearly threw up—Atticus de Loughrey, CEO.

Chief Executive Officer.

The highest-ranking person in the company.

Oh my God, I slept with the CEO of the de Loughrey Corporation!

It wasn't a thought of excitement, but fear and confusion. How did I not know? I tried to think back on all the magazines I'd seen with the family faces, but most of the faces that graced the covers were the women in the family, and not always for the right reasons.

She opened the door and my heart stopped at the sight of him behind a large wooden executive desk.

Holly smiled at me, but I could feel the blood draining from my face as I willed my feet to move.

"Mr. de Loughrey, Miss Evans for you."

He didn't look up, only nodded. "Thank you, Holly." A few keystrokes, and then his gaze skipped right past me to the wall behind me. "On time. Good."

"What is this all about, Mr. *de Loughrey?*" I accentuated his name. As far as I was aware, nobody at the restaurant knew who he was, other than an investor.

"Good morning, Miss Evans," he greeted, mimicking my use of his last name. "I trust you had no issues downstairs?"

"None," I said. "A little surprised, especially with all that we've been through."

"You didn't need my last name to enjoy my cock, if I remember."

I folded my arms over my chest, ignoring his gesture to the chairs in front of him. I wanted to get to the point of what this was all about.

"Is that why I'm here? My birthday is coming up, though this year I think I'll pass on your cock."

The grin that spread over his face made me shiver. "You're making me want to change your mind on that, but giving you multiple mind-blowing orgasms is not the reason I've brought you here today. I have a business proposition for you."

Business? "I'm not sure I'm inclined to listen to it."

"It involves an eight-figure payout."

I froze, my gaze stuck to the left of him, on the New York City skyline beyond that large floor-to-ceiling window.

Eight figures? For that amount of money, I could completely change my life. Get out of this hellhole of a city, away from my family, and start over. The problem was, who did he want me to kill for that amount?

Slowly I turned to meet his steely gaze that was pinned on me. "If it involves anything sexual, you can forget about it."

"What it involves would only be sexual if you want it to." His gaze roamed down my body, then back up, his lip twitching up. "I would not be opposed at all."

I narrowed my gaze. Yep, back to killing people. That was what people paid that kind of money for, right? Sex and death?

"What do you want then?"

"Sit." He gestured again to one of the button-back leather chairs that sat opposite his large executive desk. With a sigh, I sat, crossing my arms in front of me.

"Before we begin, I need you to sign this." He slid a piece of paper and a pen my way.

"What is it?"

"A non-disclosure agreement. You will never speak to anyone about what we talk about today."

My stomach clenched again. He was getting legal about a conversation? Our eyes were locked for a moment, neither moving before I leaned forward. My eyes scanned the page and found nothing amiss but a standard NDA.

With a quick swipe of a pen, my lips were sealed.

Once completed, he took a photo with his phone before turning his attention back to me. "I'm in need of a proxy."

"What is that?"

He twirled his hand in the air. "A stand-in, or in regard to this matter, a temporary."

"For what?"

"The future Mrs. de Loughrey."

I shook my head. "You're not making any sense."

"And I quite possibly won't until you agree. Right now, all you need to understand is that in exchange for five years of your life, I will give you ten million dollars. Plus clothes and food and all the necessities, of course. The ten million is your flat fee."

Ten million? "Dollars?"

"Yes, dollars."

"What do I have to do?"

"Marry me and bear me a child."

I blinked at him, trying to process what the hell was going on. Was I being punked? Was this a rich asshole practical joke? Was there some bet for a dollar between him and his brother to see if I'd fall for such an insane idea?

"You want to marry me?" It was the most screwed-up proposal I'd ever imagined and would forever go down in history as the first marriage proposal I received. I wasn't even going to touch the "bear me a child" part yet.

"Yes."

A laugh sprung from me, but his serious expression brought me to a halt. "You're joking, right?"

"I don't joke."

Fuck. He was serious.

I rolled over the basics again in my head—five years, ten million dollars, one child. Too good to be true, especially with his looks and status. What did he need some broke girl from Brooklyn for?

"What's the catch?"

"There are a few, but they aren't what you are thinking. We will be married in January, and hopefully, a year later, you will birth my first heir. If a second one happens in the timeframe, all the better. Once the five years are over, you are free to do whatever you like."

I blinked at him in complete confusion. None of it made sense. He had money, lots of it—tons—and because of that, coupled with his good looks, and he could have any woman he desired, so I was back to *why me?*

No, there was something weird going on.

"And *why* do you think I'd even contemplate agreeing to this insane idea? Buying me to be your wife?"

"Because I'm offering you a life you could only dream of and a payout that will possibly ensure you never have to work again."

"This is a heavy proposal," I said as it began to sink in.

"The fact that you are still sitting in front of me gives me hope you are entertaining the idea of becoming my wife. I will stress, this is a one-time-only offer. You will, of course, have some time to think it over, but after that, if you decide to decline, then later change your mind, it's off the table."

"How much time?"

"I'll see you back here at the same time tomorrow."

I stood, my mind whirling. "I'll see you tomorrow then."

"Before you go," he said, stopping me from walking

away. "I will remind you to remain silent on this matter. Speak to no one about what we have discussed."

I nodded and swallowed. As if anyone would believe me anyway. The idea was ludicrous. So out there, even I was having difficulty believing it was real.

I also would never tell anyone because I knew the de Loughreys had the backing to sue me for all the money I would ever make in this life and the next if I broke the agreement. You didn't cross them, or you paid the price—and it wasn't always money.

A leather binder was placed in front of me, one of those legal ones that opened at the top, and pressed into the tightly bound hide was the de Loughrey logo.

"This is the preliminary contract. Look it over, and we can discuss any issues in the morning."

I numbly nodded, suddenly having a strange out-of-body experience as the weight of reality pressed down upon me. After slipping the document in my bag, I turned to leave.

"Nine sharp," he said as I gripped the door handle. I turned to look back at him, our gazes locked as I exited.

Autopilot drove me to the train station, and I stared blankly in front of me. On the one hand, I should have been insulted. On the other hand—ten million dollars.

Could I stand five years with him? He was a busy man, so technically, I wouldn't see him much, right?

Selling myself as a fake wife. Could I do it, pretend to be something I wasn't, act like a doting wife to a man like Atticus de Loughrey? *Be* a de Loughrey?

Those were the thoughts that had my heart slamming in my chest.

Atticus represented everything that was wrong with the world. Greed and privilege, patriarchy and the belief that women are nothing but holes to fuck. And I hated that, but not as much as I hated myself for wanting a taste of him again.

It would be a life most only dreamed about, but was it something I wanted? More than that, was it something I could even do?

Could I really kneel before the king?

Continue reading here

about THE AUTHOR

K.I. Lynn is the USA Today Bestselling Author from The Bend Anthology and the Amazon Bestsellers, Breach and Becoming Mrs Lockwood. She spent her life in the arts, everything from music to painting and ceramics, then to writing. Characters have always run around in her head, acting out their stories, but it wasn't until later in life she would put them to pen. It would turn out to be the one thing she was really passionate about.

Since she began posting stories online, she's garnered acclaim for her diverse stories and hard hitting writing style. Two stories and characters are never the same, her brain moving through different ideas faster than she can write them down as it also plots its quest for world domination…or cheese. Whichever is easier to obtain… Usually it's cheese.

Website—www.kilynnauthor.com
Facebook—http://bit.ly/1qbp5tx
Twitter—https://twitter.com/KI_Lynn_
Instagram—https://www.instagram.com/k.i.lynn
Get my Newsletter—http://bit.ly/1U9NSoC

<p style="text-align:center;">more books from
K.I. LYNN

Wicked Rule

I'm going to make her my queen.

One wedding.

One child.

Five years.

Ten million dollars.

Those are the terms of our contract.

My offer is sound, bold, and necessary. In order to gain my inheritance, I have to have a wife.

She thinks her clause will keep me from having her skin on mine.

She's very wrong.

The de Loughrey's rule the world, and I am their king. I get what I want, and what I want is her.

I'll have her beneath me no matter what.

Find out more here—books2read.com/WickedRule

Ruthless Rule

They call me the ruthless ruler…and they're not wrong.

In the boardroom and the bedroom I take no prisoners and when I'm done, it's all stop.

There's something about my father's new assistant and a chance encounter brings us closer than I ever expected. Once isn't enough, but for the first time in my life, I'm shot down.

Me.

A de Loughrey.

So I sweeten it with money. An indecent proposal that gives both of what we need.

When I learn her secrets I find the impossible bloom inside me.

I'm the ruthless ruler, but she has me by the heart.

Business is business, and when it's done, I don't know what will happen to the heart she holds.

I've met my ruthless match.

Find out more here—books2read.com/RuthlessRule

Off the Cuff

I spilled a cup of coffee on the President of Acquisitions.

He deserved it.

Not the brightest idea, but I'd had a bad day, and now he's getting back at me.

For nine weeks I'm to be his assistant, and there's nothing I can do about it.

It's punishment.

Every moment we're near each other it's a constant battle of wills, but I refuse to go down.

If only my fantasies didn't invade our arguments.

If only he wasn't so good looking.

Everything is off the cuff, including him pinning me to the wall.

Now he wants something else from me.

A date.

There's just one problem—he doesn't know I have a child.

Find out more here—books2read.com/ThatNightKILynn

That Night

I got pregnant on New Year's Eve.

That night was hands down the best night of my life. A magical night with the man of my dreams.

The aftermath changed everything.

After weeks of silence from him and a positive pregnancy test, it was safe to say I was in full out panic mode.

Until I walked into a conference room only to find Mr. Man-of-my-dreams-father-of-my-unborn-child at the head of the table.

Turns out the VP of finance isn't an old boring guy with white hair.

Two different cities.

A baby on the way.

An intense attraction.

And he's technically my boss.

Life just got even more complicated.

Find out more here—books2read.com/ThatNightKILynn

Domenico

The mafia never lets you go.

I thought I was safe, free, but I never expected to find myself
locked in a cage.

I'm in his territory. His prison.

The beast.

A fate worse than death awaits me if I can't get away, so
when the opportunity of salvation presents itself I grab it,
even if I'm unsure if I can trust the hand I'm holding.

The only way out is through, exposing secrets and spilling
blood.

Things aren't how they appear. Nobody is what they seem.

Not even me.

Welcome to the Cameo Hotel

I get what I want.

When I walked through the door of the Cameo Hotel I didn't expect such a beauty to be working the front desk.

The effect she has on me is intense, and I make her life a living hell because of it.

I love her spirit, her internal defiance when completing the most inane task I assign her. My two week stay has turned into unending, just to be near her.

She's under my every command if she wants to keep me happy.

There's one last thing I want.

Her.

Find out more here
books2read.com/WelcomeToTheCameoHotel

Becoming Mrs. Lockwood

Every girl has dreams of meeting Prince Charming, or at least I know I did.

A fairy tale-like meeting of love at first site.

Real life and fairy tales are very different.

I'm just a small town Indiana girl that had a chance encounter with one of Hollywood's golden boys. You may think you know where this story goes—not even close.

Life is different. Marriage is hard. It's even worse when you're strangers.

Find out more here
books2read.com/BecomingMrsLockwood

Six

I had a one-night stand. It wasn't my first, but it would be my last.

A gun to the head.

A trained killer.

A deadly conspiracy.

Kidnapped and on the run, my life and death is in the hands of a sadist captor who happens to be my one-night stand. Armed with countless weapons, money, and new identities, the man I call Six drags me around the world.

The manhunt is on and Six is the next target. Can we find out who is killing off the Cleaners before they find us?

Two down, seven to go.

When it's all over he'll finish the job that dropped him into my life, and end it.

Stockholm Syndrome meets bucket list, and the question of what would you do to live before you died. The questions aren't always answered in black and white. Gray becomes the norm as my morals are tested.

Death is a tragedy, and I'll do anything to stay alive.

Are you ready for the last ride of your life? Six has a gun to your head—what would you do?

This isn't a love story.

It's a death story.

Breach Book 1

His body was sin, his cock was sin, and I was a sinner.

To keep myself safe I hide in the world and let life move around me.

My new partner, Nathan, isn't safe. Far from it.

The darkness coils around him, hidden by a shield created by a blinding smile. But those who live in shadows see past the façade we create.

Even in darkness, there is light. A spark that ignites, then explodes.

Every filthy word from his mouth, every possessive touch—I crave them, need them. Violent and passionate and everything I need to fill the void inside me, but one thing is missing.

He can never love me.

More than my heart is on the line, and I don't know if I'll survive our breach.

Find out more here—books2read.com/Breach

The Executive

Business is king, and I have an empire to topple.

Ivy is my new assistant and a threat to me. She's my undoing. If ever I was to believe in a cosmic connection, it was the moment I met her.

For years I've had one goal—revenge. As CEO, I have crafted a strategic plan for business, but never a life beyond.

With one touch from her, the veil is lifted. Things are different, and every moment I'm near her, my world begins to change.

A wall of propriety keeps me from her. I need her as my pawn in this war, beside me in battle. Sharing the secrets of my enemies, and her desires in my bed. Her body to claim as mine.

Getting what I want has consequences.

Collateral damage is real.

In the game of crushing kings of men, I never planned on my heart being a sacrifice.

Find out more here—books2read.com/TheExecutive

Cocksure

Co-written with Olivia Kelley

A life altering lie, ten years, and one wild night later, the
game has changed.

Niko

My life is great. I love my job, have awesome friends, and a
great family.

Women love me, even if they know it's just for a night.

I always thought love at first sight was bullshit. Then she
came storming into my life. She tore through my every rule,
rocked my world, and knocked me on my ass.

There's only one problem…she lied.+

Turns out my best friend's little sister isn't so little anymore.

Everly

I stole a night with my fantasy. Lied to him.

After ten years of not seeing each other, Niko doesn't even
recognize me.

So I take what I want from him, what I need from him.
Without worry. Without consequence.

What I didn't count on was the lingering need for him.

Once the truth is out, the game changes. There are consequences.

I should have known nothing in my life is ever simple.

My brother is going to kill his best friend and I have nine months to figure out what I want.

Find out more here
books2read.com/Cocksure-Lynn-Kelley

Need Book 1

Co-written with N. Isabelle Blanco

I was Kira's from the first moment I saw her. Maybe it was love at first sight, but I was only ten.

She became my best friend.

My crush.

The girl I can't live without.

But I have to.

She was almost mine, but my father took away my chance.

Now she lives across the hall from me. Instead of the title of girlfriend, she's now my stepsister.

But that doesn't stop how I feel, how I want her. Thankfully, I'm off to college two hundred miles away, but even that doesn't help.

She's under my skin, all around me, and I watch her morph from a sexy teenager to an irresistible woman.

I can't take it anymore, I need her.

Is it possible to ever be happy without the one person you *need?*

"I'm Brayden, baby. The man you've been dreaming about your whole life. And I'm about to fucking show you why."

Part 1 of a 3 part series.

Find out more here—books2read.com/NeedSeries